Silver Dolphins

MOONLIGHT MAGIC

DISCARD

For Zara, Naomi and Alicia

*With thanks to Pat, Claire, Catherine, Lizzie
and Rachel for all their support and hard work.*

First published in paperback by HarperCollins *Children's Books* in 2009

HarperCollins *Children's Books* is a division of HarperCollins*Publishers* Ltd,
77-85 Fulham Palace Road, Hammersmith, London W6 8JB.

Visit our website at: www.harpercollins.co.uk

1 3 5 7 9 10 8 6 4 2
ISBN-13: 978-0-00-730973-3

A CIP catalogue record for this title is available from the British Library.
All rights reserved.

Typeset by Palimpsest Book Production Limited, Grangemouth, Stirlingshire
Printed and bound in England by Clays Ltd, St Ives plc

by Summer Waters

Silver Dolphins

MOONLIGHT MAGIC

HarperCollins *Children's Books*

Prologue

Spirit, the dolphin leader with a striking yellow blaze that stretched along his flank, banged his tail in the water for silence. At once, the thirty dolphins milling in the sea stopped chattering and turned to face him. Spirit bowed his magnificent head.

"I'm going away on a very long journey. Star, my wife, will be in charge until I return."

"Where are you going, Dad?" A small dolphin with a cheeky face asked the question on everyone's mind.

Spirit smiled indulgently at his son, Bubbles.

"The Silver Dolphins are leaving us. I have

to arrange for their talents to be put to good use elsewhere."

As one, the dolphins clicked their surprise.

"Why do the Silver Dolphins have to leave?" asked Bubbles, his bright eyes suddenly anxious. "Will they come back again?"

"The Silver Dolphins have a very special journey to make, but yes, they will return."

"But I don't want them to go away." Bubbles was upset and indignant.

Spirit gave him a reassuring smile. "We don't own the Silver Dolphins and they don't own us. All creatures should be free to do as they wish. Let someone go and one day they will return. Keep them against their will and they will always hold it against you."

The dolphins were silent as they digested

Spirit's wise words. Then Bubbles squeaked, "The Silver Dolphins must go on their journey. Tell them I said that, Dad, so they'll come back to me."

There were loud clicks of laughter. Affectionately, Spirit patted Bubbles's head with a flipper.

"You can tell them yourself," he answered. "Before I go I have a small job for the Silver Dolphins. Hush now and let me call them."

Chapter One

There was no mistaking the tall, athletic-looking man coming towards Antonia and Cai in the airport terminal. He had the same dark, curly hair and laughing brown eyes as Cai.

"Dad!" cried Cai. "Mum!" He threw himself at his parents, hugging them both.

Antonia caught her breath, suddenly feeling

shy and a little homesick. She wished her parents were here in Australia too. But that was unfair. It had been almost two months since Cai had seen his mum and dad, who were working in Australia while Cai stayed in England with his Great Aunty Claudia. This was a big moment for him.

Angela Pacific, a slim lady with pretty blonde hair, broke away from the group. "Hello, you must be Antonia. We've heard so much about you. It's great to meet you at last."

"Thanks," mumbled Antonia shyly.

"Antonia!" cried Lenny Pacific, encompassing her with his free arm and almost hugging the breath out of her. "You are going to *love* Australia."

"Right now I expect she'd love to get to the

apartment," said Mrs Pacific, smiling. "We've a car outside. It's about sixty kilometres to the hotel complex we've booked for your stay, but it shouldn't take long at this time of night."

Antonia was grateful to relax and let Cai's parents organise things. It had been a long journey, two whole days since she'd left home to fly around the world for a ten-day holiday with Cai. The airline had put a very motherly lady in charge of them, but it wasn't the same as travelling with your own family. It was much nicer having Cai's parents to help with the bags and find the way to the car park.

While Mr Pacific loaded the suitcases into the boot of the hire car, Cai and Antonia climbed into the back. Once they got on to the highway, Mr Pacific switched on the air conditioning and

Antonia gratefully sank back in her seat. That felt better. It was as warm as a sunny day in England even though it must be gone midnight. Antonia didn't bother to look at her watch, knowing it was still on English time.

"The place we're living in only has one bedroom, so we've rented a holiday apartment in the grounds of a brand-new hotel complex." Mrs Pacific twisted round in her seat so she could talk to Antonia and Cai. "It's right next to the beach. We know how much you love the water, Cai, and Claudia tells us that Antonia's the same. She made me promise to book a seaside location to keep you both happy."

The friends exchanged a secret smile. There was a reason for Cai and Antonia's shared love of the sea. Unconsciously, Antonia's hand strayed to the dolphin charm she always wore round her neck.

She and Cai were Silver Dolphins, or guardians of the sea. They had special magical abilities to help them care for the oceans and the creatures living there. Silver Dolphins were rare. Only someone who was in tune with nature and believed in magic could become one. Claudia had been a Silver Dolphin once, although these days she ran a marine conservation charity called Sea Watch.

Antonia closed her eyes, drifting in and out of sleep as the car sped along the empty roads. Then Cai gently shook her arm.

"We're here," he said.

The hotel complex looked like a small city

with so many lights blazing against the inky black sky. Antonia pressed her nose up to the window for a better look.

"Wow!"

"Isn't it amazing?" said Mr Pacific. He slowed the car as the buildings drew closer, then turned right and parked outside a neat row of bungalows. "It's got everything. Three pools, two hot tubs, a gym, tennis courts, a cinema…"

"Darling, you sound like a holiday brochure," interrupted Mrs Pacific. "Let's get these poor children to bed and they can explore for themselves tomorrow."

Sleepily, Antonia and Cai followed Mr and Mrs Pacific into the holiday apartment. It was the nicest place Antonia had ever stayed in and had three bedrooms and two bathrooms. Antonia and Cai's rooms were next door to each other. The spacious lounge had patio doors and a tiny modern kitchen and dining area at one end.

Antonia stood at the doors, staring into the night. The patio was lit by soft garden lights. Beyond it was a balcony overlooking the sea. A huge moon hung in the sky and the water sparkled like black diamonds.

"I can't wait to go swimming," said Cai, yawning.

"Me too," agreed Antonia, although right now she was too tired to do anything. Mrs Pacific let Antonia telephone her mum and dad to tell them she'd arrived safely. It felt funny knowing they were so far away. Antonia

was too tired to talk for long and promised to phone back when she was more awake.

"Bedtime," said Mrs Pacific, when Antonia came off the phone.

Gratefully, Antonia followed her to the bedroom where Mr Pacific had put her suitcase and bag. She looked around, taking in the single bed, wardrobe, dressing table and wall-mounted television.

"If you need anything in the night, just ask." Mrs Pacific smiled at Antonia then, blowing her a kiss, closed the door.

Antonia pulled her pyjamas out of the suitcase. It was an effort to undress and she left her clothes in an untidy heap. Without bothering to brush her hair or teeth, she peeled back the duvet and climbed into bed. Bliss! She reached for the bedside light to turn it off then stopped. On the wall opposite the bed hung a picture of three dolphins, their gleaming bodies almost vertical as they leapt out of the sea.

Antonia stared at the picture for a moment. The dolphins were bottlenoses, unlike her own pod of common dolphins. Antonia felt a sharp pang of homesickness. What had she done? She'd left her mum, dad and little sister Jessica, and her wonderful dolphins, Spirit, Star, Dream and Bubbles, to travel to the other side of the world and stay with people she hardly knew.

Antonia had been very worried about leaving the dolphins. What if they needed help while she and Cai were away? But Claudia had promised that she would answer their call.

"I'm not that ancient that I can't fill in for

you both for a couple of weeks!" she'd said indignantly.

Antonia's fingers curled round her dolphin charm. It felt soft and slippery, just like a real dolphin. Slowly her anxiety slipped away. She hadn't travelled to Australia alone. She was here with Cai, and if his parents were as nice as he was then she would have a wonderful time. Cai was the brave one. When he'd first come to Sandy Bay, he'd not known anyone apart from his Great Aunty Claudia, whom he'd only visited a few times.

Switching off the light, Antonia snuggled down in bed. The moment her eyes closed she saw dolphins. She slept soundly and dreamt she was playing a game of Sprat with Bubbles, Dream and Cai.

Chapter Two

Antonia woke with the sun on her face. It was filtering in from a different direction than she was used to and for a second she couldn't work out where she was. She opened her eyes and saw three leaping dolphins on the wall opposite. Suddenly everything came back in a rush. She was in Australia with Cai!

At once Antonia jumped out of bed and rummaged through her suitcase for shorts and a T-shirt. Finding her washbag, she pulled out a hairbrush and combed the tangles from her long blonde hair.

On her way to the bathroom she bumped into Cai, still in his pyjamas.

"Hi," he yawned sleepily. "Mum's making us brunch."

Antonia's stomach grumbled hungrily, making them both laugh.

"I'll just have a quick wash," she said.

"No hurry," said Cai, yawning again. "Suppose I'd better get dressed."

Cai took ages and eventually Antonia gave up hovering outside his room and went in search of his parents. They were in the kitchen, where Mr Pacific was cutting up a fresh pineapple while Mrs Pacific fried bacon.

"Hi, did you sleep well?"

"Yes, thanks. Can I do anything?" Antonia felt awkward watching Cai's parents doing all the work.

"You could put the plates on the patio table. We're eating outside." Mrs Pacific pointed her spatula in the direction of the plates then expertly flipped the bacon over. It sizzled and spat and Antonia's stomach growled again.

"Hungry?" Mrs Pacific smiled.

"Very," said Antonia, suddenly feeling more relaxed.

She carried the plates outside then leant on the balcony, taking in the view. It was magnificent. The hotel gardens dropped steeply down to the beach about three metres beneath her. The golden sand, dotted with scrubby vegetation and palms, was fringed by crystal blue sea.

Dazzled by its brightness, Antonia screwed up her eyes. It was so hot. Guiltily, she remembered her sun hat and suncream were still somewhere in her suitcase. Mum had made her promise to wear both whenever she went outside.

But before she could fetch them, Cai and his parents came out, carrying trays of food and drink. While Mrs Pacific arranged the food on the table, Mr Pacific erected a sun umbrella. Thankfully it gave plenty of shade so Antonia stopped worrying about suncream and sat down to eat. It was one of the best meals she had ever tasted. There was a fresh tropical-fruit salad, club sandwiches bursting with bacon, prawn salad sandwiches and ice-cold mango and orange smoothies.

"We're planning a few trips out," said Mrs Pacific, helping herself to a large bowl of fruit salad. "And there's plenty to do here in the hotel complex. Why don't you spend today exploring? The pools all have lifeguards so you can swim whenever you like."

"Great," said Cai. "I'd love a swim. What about you, Antonia?"

"Yes," said Antonia decisively. It was so hot she could happily spend all day in the pool.

"Sounds fun," said Mr Pacific. "I might swim too. You two go for a wander while we clear up. I'll come and find you later by one of the pools."

"Are you sure? I don't mind helping with the washing up," said Antonia, pushing back her chair. Was it her imagination or did the tail of her dolphin charm twitch just then?

"Thanks, but there's a dishwasher," said Mrs Pacific, chuckling. "That was one of my holiday requests! Tonight we're eating in the hotel restaurant. There's an outdoor one overlooking the beach. It's wonderful and has great food."

Antonia couldn't wait to explore. Quickly she went to her room to put on suncream and get her hat. As she rubbed the cream into her arms, the dolphin picture caught her eye. It was a stunning photo. The leaping dolphins reminded her of Bubbles when he did the twister: a full circle standing on the sea on his tail.

Suddenly Antonia had a very strong feeling that the dolphins needed her. She raised a hand to touch her charm, but stopped when she remembered her fingers were covered with sticky suncream. The dolphin charm began to vibrate, softly at first, then more rapidly.

Antonia was so surprised she stood rooted to the spot. Spirit knew she wasn't in Sandy Bay, so who was calling to her? An ear-splitting whistle rang round the room.

Silver Dolphin, we need you.

I hear your call. Antonia automatically answered the unfamiliar voice in her head.

She wiped her hands clean and ran to the door. At the same time Cai shot out of his room. His brown eyes were wide with shock.

"Is that Spirit?" he asked.

"No," said Antonia, who was a more powerful Silver Dolphin than Cai and could communicate with Spirit telepathically. "But we still have to answer the call."

"I know," said Cai.

Shouting a hasty goodbye to his parents, Cai opened the apartment door and ran outside. At the end of the road, past the last bungalow apartment, was a flight of steps with an arrow pointing to the beach.

Antonia and Cai sprinted over to the stone steps, which were steep and twisty. Clutching the metal handrail for support, they scrambled down them until they reached the hotel's private beach. It was packed with holiday-makers enjoying a day in the sun.

Antonia and Cai were used to making

themselves invisible in crowded places. They left their shoes under a low, prickly bush at the furthest end of the beach and ran across the golden sand. As they splashed into the water, Antonia caught her breath in surprise. The sea was lovely and warm! She waded out until it was deep enough to swim before diving into the clear blue water. Immediately her legs melded together, kicking the water like a dolphin's tail.

Hurry, Silver Dolphin.

The charm thrummed urgently against her neck.

I'm coming.

Using her hands like flippers, Antonia sliced through the water. Her arching body leapt in and out of the sea like a real dolphin. She swam for ages, conscious only of the call of the dolphin and Cai racing along beside her. When the hotel beach was a small speck in the distance, Antonia felt vibrations in the water. They grew stronger until at last she saw a magnificent bottlenose dolphin swimming towards her.

The dolphin stopped a tail's length away, mouth open slightly, showing a neat row of small white teeth. For a split second Antonia thought the dolphin was laughing, but realised that there was no laughter in those dark eyes. She hesitated, wondering if she should greet the dolphin by rubbing noses like she did with Spirit.

Then the dolphin clicked, "Thank you for answering my call, Silver Dolphins. We urgently need your help. Please follow me."

Chapter Three

"My name is Diamond. I'm the leader of a pod of bottlenose dolphins that live here in Blue Reef Bay," explained the dolphin as she sped along. "We heard there were Silver Dolphins in the area. You've come at a good time. There's a lot for you to do."

Antonia was thrilled, but astonished. Did

news spread as fast in the dolphin world as it did in hers? Had Spirit arranged for them to work with Diamond or had the bottle-nosed leader sensed their presence? That was the wonderful thing about magic, Antonia decided. It was full of surprises.

"How can we help?" she clicked.

"There's a turtle caught in a fishing net. We're nearly there."

A turtle! In spite of the warm water, Antonia shivered. Discarded fishing nets were a common problem and often proved deadly. She swam faster, anxious to help the endangered creature.

Diamond began to swim towards the shore. The hotel beach lay to the left then the coastline dipped inwards forming a small secluded bay. The beach was beautiful with golden sand and a fringe of palm trees at the furthest end. Soon Diamond slowed.

"It's too shallow for me to go any closer," she clicked. "I'll wait here. Hurry, Silver Dolphins."

Side by side, Antonia and Cai swam towards the beach. Antonia saw the turtle first and she cried out in horror. "Oh, the poor thing!"

The green turtle was almost a metre long and completely trussed up in a bright blue fishing net. He lay in the shallows, like a huge bundle of rubbish, the sea gently rocking him back and forth. The tip of his front flippers protruded from the netting, but he was too tangled up to move them.

Antonia looked around for something sharp

to cut the net with. There was nothing in the water, but the beach was peppered with small stones. She and Cai ran up the beach to look for a largish stone with a sharp edge.

When they got back in the water, Antonia realised the stone she had chosen was next to useless, having little effect on the thick blue netting. Cai was having similar problems with his too. They stood on either side of the turtle, desperately sawing at the rope.

"This is going to take ages," grunted Cai.

"We need something sharper," Antonia agreed.

She concentrated on one square of the net at a time, hooking the stone under it, then sawing upwards. She didn't think she would harm the turtle's thick brown shell, but she was careful not to scratch it or to nick his leathery limbs. Very slowly the netting began to fall away and as the turtle found he could move, he panicked, thrashing his flippers and long tail. Antonia sawed faster, worried that he might hurt himself.

Cut the net, she urged, as if the stone could hear her thoughts. The turtle lashed out, almost knocking it from Antonia's hand. She stumbled, then recovering her balance, stood with her feet further apart. In her mind she imagined the stone cutting through the rope as easily as if it was butter.

Suddenly, a warm feeling spread down Antonia's hand and into her fingers. The stone grew almost too hot to hold. Antonia's grey-green eyes widened. *What was happening?*

She usually had this sensation when she was healing an injured animal. Fingers tingling, she pressed the stone against the net.

Cut, she thought.

Immediately the stone slid through the rope. Antonia tackled a new section of net. Again the stone cut through it with ease. With growing excitement, Antonia worked faster. She was vaguely aware of Cai watching her, his face a mixture of amazement and pride. Soon only the turtle's hind flippers and tail were caught in the net. He tried to swim away, dragging the net behind him.

"Steady," soothed Cai. Gently he laid a hand on the turtle's head. "Don't panic. You'll soon be free."

His calm manner worked like a dream. The

turtle stopped struggling and turned his head to watch Cai with one oval-shaped eye. As the last piece of rope fell away, Antonia stood back, pushing the hair out of her eyes with a relieved sigh.

"We did it!" she exclaimed.

The tingly sensation had faded, leaving her hands as limp as washed-up seaweed. She watched the turtle strike out for freedom. He swam gracefully, his scaly neck outstretched as he propelled himself forward.

"Well done!" Cai turned to Antonia, eyes shining. "That was so cool. I never knew you could do that."

"Me neither," Antonia confessed. Longingly, she looked at the beach. It was so tempting to go and sit on the soft golden sand. She

felt completely drained now the rescue was over.

"You can see the hotel from here," said Cai. "It really spoils the view. Hey! Look over there…" His voice suddenly rose with excitement as a large lizard-like creature scuttled across the beach and disappeared behind the trees.

"What was that?" Antonia was glad she was safely in the sea.

"I think it was a goanna. They're a type of lizard common in Australia. They eat baby turtles." Cai started to go after it.

"I like turtles much better than goannas," said Antonia with feeling. "They're incredible and so dignified. Cai, where are you going? Diamond's waiting for us."

Cai stopped splashing towards the shore

and turned back with a guilty grin. "Whoops! I almost forgot."

Antonia laughed then suddenly feeling vibrations in the shallow water, she spun round.

"More dolphins! I bet they're from Diamond's pod." She pointed to a small group of dolphins hovering out at sea.

"Wicked!" exclaimed Cai. "Let's go say hello."

Antonia counted five dolphins. There was Diamond, swimming a little apart from the rest of the group, two other adults and two younger dolphins. The littlest one was a bit larger than Bubbles and Antonia momentarily felt a flash of homesickness as she remembered her favourite dolphin friend.

The dolphins whistled a greeting as Antonia and Cai swam over. Diamond opened her mouth and clicked a laugh.

"Everyone's so excited. You're our first Silver Dolphins."

"Hello," clicked Antonia.

Diamond swam forwards and, dipping her elegant head, greeted Antonia and Cai with a friendly nose rub.

"Welcome to Blue Reef Bay," she whistled. "There wasn't time to say it before, but it's an honour to have you here."

Chapter Four

Diamond had brought her closest family to meet the Silver Dolphins.

"This is my sister, Beauty, and her husband, Blaze," she clicked.

The two adult dolphins dipped their silver grey heads.

"And their children, Jet and Swirl."

The younger dolphins swam forward and high-fived Antonia and Cai with a fin.

"Can we play with the Silver Dolphins?" Jet asked.

"Please, Aunty Diamond?" squeaked Swirl.

Diamond clicked a laugh. "If the Silver Dolphins want to," she replied.

"We'd love to," clicked Antonia.

"Bubbly!" Swirl smacked her tail in the water.

Beauty and Blaze had lots of questions to ask the Silver Dolphins first, and Antonia was conscious of Jet and Swirl impatiently bobbing in the water as she and Cai answered them. At last the adults swam away.

"Thank goodness," clicked Jet impatiently. "Let's play Sprat. I'll be it. It's a two-wave head start."

Swirl and Cai immediately dived under the water, leaving Antonia on her own. When they played Sprat with Bubbles and Dream, they always gave each other a three-wave head start.

"Two waves," whistled Jet, smacking his tail on the water. "Ready or not, I'm coming!"

Quickly, Antonia dived into the crystal clear ocean. Beneath her the sandy seabed stretched for miles. There was nowhere to hide yet Cai and Swirl had completely disappeared. A bubble of panic rose in Antonia's chest. Where were they?

She could feel Jet swimming after her, his vibrations growing stronger as he closed the distance between them. Antonia was fast in the water, but today she felt like she was swimming in syrup. It was a struggle to go anywhere. She kicked her tail-like legs, forcing her body on. Then something butted against her foot.

"Sprat!" clicked Jet triumphantly. "You're it."

Deftly, he somersaulted and swam in the opposite direction, leaving Antonia wondering how she'd been caught so easily. She turned slowly, like a cumbersome ocean liner, and gave chase. Jet was way ahead, a silver-grey missile hurtling through the sea. Antonia hurried after him, but her limbs felt so clumsy that the effort of swimming made them ache.

She wished she hadn't agreed to play Sprat. All she really wanted to do was to lie in the shade and sleep. Her eyes drooped at the thought and she jerked them open. *What was happening to her? Why did she feel like this?*

I'm being a wuss! she thought and with a wry smile Antonia forced herself on. She was determined to make a good impression on Jet and Swirl so they would want to play with her again.

After swimming for a while, Antonia saw a dark cluster of rocks ahead. It had to be where everyone was hiding. Silently, she swam closer, and when she was a tail's length away, three shapes broke cover and swam in the opposite direction.

Squeaking with surprise, Antonia paddled after Cai, but for once she couldn't catch him. The gap between them was widening when a shoal of exotic fish flittered past. Cai hesitated, staring at the fish in delight. Taking advantage of his momentary loss of concentration,

Antonia surged forward and tagged him on the hand.

"Sprat!" she panted.

"Aw!" squeaked Cai. "Not fair! I got distracted."

"Tough!" said Antonia heartlessly.

She swam away from Cai, but her limbs felt like lead and it was a relief when Jet called an end to the game with a massive water fight. Jet was even more skilful at water fights than Bubbles. He was excellent at breaching – launching himself out of the water then crashing back down to cause a colossal splash.

"That's so cool!" said Cai, his eyes shining. "Will you teach me how to breach?"

"It's easy," clicked Jet. "I'll show you now if you like."

"Not today. We'd better get back before

we're missed." Antonia hoped she didn't sound like a spoilsport and was relieved when Cai agreed with her.

"You're right. Dad's expecting to meet us by the pool."

"Next time then," said Jet, with a mischievous twinkle in his eye. "Then we'll have a water fight. You and me against the girls."

"I want to learn breaching too," clicked Antonia indignantly.

"Don't worry," said Swirl. "I'll teach you."

"Thanks, Swirl." Antonia rubbed noses with her new friend, then she rubbed noses with Jet while Cai and Swirl said goodbye.

"See you soon, Silver Dolphins."

Jet and Swirl swam out to sea, their silver grey bodies glittering in the sun.

"Let's find Dad," said Cai when the dolphins were tiny specks in the distance. "I can't wait to try out the hotel pools. One of them has a wicked water slide."

"Sounds fun," panted Antonia.

"Are you all right?" Cai slowed to wait for her to catch up.

"I'm fine. I just feel really tired."

"Jet lag," said Cai knowingly. "It happens when you fly across different time zones. Your body has difficulty working it out and it makes you feel tired all the time."

"How come you haven't got it then?"

"I am a bit tired," Cai admitted. "But some people get jet lag worse than others."

They swam ashore in silence. As they rose out of the sea, the water poured off them like a waterfall, leaving their clothes completely dry. The only sign that they'd been swimming was their slightly damp hair, but that soon dried in the hot Australian sun. Antonia pulled at a thin strand of seaweed caught on her T-shirt and tossed it back into the sea.

"We've come ashore in the wrong place," said Cai. "Our shoes are over that way."

They walked in the surf, enjoying the feel of the warm water splashing around their ankles.

"Look at that," said Antonia crossly. She stooped to pick up an empty drinks can bobbing towards the beach.

"Stop! Don't touch that!"

A tall man wearing swimming trunks and mirrored sunglasses shouted at Antonia and began to make his way over towards them.

Chapter Five

A tiny wave pushed the drinks can on to the sand, then another wave pulled it back into the sea. Antonia's face flamed with embarrassment as she watched it. Why was the man so angry? She hadn't thrown the can away!

The man ran towards her, stopping by the

can. He pushed the sunglasses on to the top of his head and smiled.

"G'day," he drawled in a strong Australian accent. "Sorry, didn't mean to shout at you. You're not local, are you?"

"We're from England," said Antonia, conscious of her own accent.

"Cool! You're on holiday then?"

"Yes." Antonia was guarded, knowing she wasn't supposed to talk to strangers, no matter how friendly they sounded.

"You've gotta be real careful about picking up things on the beach. Cans especially make a great home for the blue ring octopus. It's a pretty little thing, but deadly. One bite from a blue ring contains enough poison to kill you."

"Oh!" Antonia jumped away from the can as if it might suddenly bite her.

The man banged his hand against his forehead. "Now I've scared you. Just be careful, that's all. Best if you leave litter picking to the clear-up team. They're on the beach every day."

He stooped down and gingerly picked up the can. "Empty," he said, peering inside. "But you never know. Have a good day."

Saluting them with his free hand, he walked away, taking the empty can with him.

Antonia stared at Cai in alarm. "No litter picking," she said weakly.

"Absolutely not," agreed Cai. "Maybe we ought to get some of those beach shoes. The ones you can wear in the sea."

"Maybe," said Antonia. "But our Silver Dolphin magic will protect us when we're in the water."

"Only if we're answering a call," said Cai.

"Good point," said Antonia, hurrying for her sandals and putting them on in double quick time.

They found Cai's dad lounging on a sunbed by the side of the largest pool. "Did you have fun exploring?" he asked.

"We did – it's a great place. The beach is fantastic," said Cai.

Mr Pacific sat up. "You went on the beach? I thought you were exploring the hotel facilities. I should have told you not to go in the sea without me or your mother."

"We won't," said Antonia guiltily, crossing

her fingers behind her back. Going in the sea to answer the dolphin's call didn't count, but she still felt bad deceiving Mr Pacific.

"Who's for a swim in the pool then?" said Mr Pacific.

"Me!" Cai shouted, pulling off his clothes to reveal a baggy pair of swimming trunks.

Yawning, Antonia sat down on a free sun lounger shaded by a colourful sun umbrella.

"No thanks. I'll sit here and watch."

"Will you be all right on your own?" Cai looked concerned.

"I'm fine." Antonia knew she sounded wimpy, but couldn't help it. She didn't have the energy to swim. "Have fun."

The pool had a water slide and Cai and his

dad took turns seeing who could make the biggest splash sliding into the water.

It was very hot. Antonia watched them longingly, wishing she had the energy to join in, but it was a struggle to keep her eyes open. She hoped it was the jet lag that had sapped her energy and not overusing her magical powers. The way they'd allowed her to cut the net from the turtle was unreal! Eventually she gave in to her sleepiness, the sounds of the pool fading as she dozed off.

Much later she woke with a dry throat and a buzzing sound in her ear. Sitting up too quickly, Antonia was overcome with dizziness and gripped the arms of the sun lounger. What was that noise? Was Diamond about to call? Unsteadily she let go of the sun lounger to touch her charm. It felt silky soft, like a real dolphin, but it wasn't vibrating.

She scanned the pool and saw Cai being pushed round by his dad on an inflatable lilo. He was laughing and splashing his dad with both hands. His silver dolphin charm, pinned to his swimming trunks, sparkled in the sunlight. It couldn't be calling to Cai or he would have made an excuse to leave the pool.

Antonia relaxed. The buzz in her ear was quieter now. She must have got water in it. She rubbed it until eventually the noise stopped. The pool looked cool and inviting. Antonia stood up, meaning to join Cai, but she still felt dizzy so she sank back on to the sun lounger. This was horrible. Hopefully, after an early night, she'd be back to her old self tomorrow.

Dinner was later than Antonia was used to. The outdoor restaurant was wonderful and the family was given a table overlooking the beach. It was incredible watching the sun slip slowly into the ocean. For some reason Antonia didn't feel hungry. She nibbled at her food, wishing she had more of an appetite, especially when the waitress brought out enormous ice-cream sundaes topped with a mountain of frothy cream, whole strawberries and strawberry sauce.

"I was going to suggest a walk along the beach after dinner, but Antonia looks half asleep," said Mrs Pacific.

Antonia sat up. "I'd love a walk," she said.

"Are you sure? I expect you're still tired from the flight."

"I am, but I'd still like a walk."

The jet lag hadn't affected Cai who had bags of energy. Antonia was frustrated with herself, but there was nothing she could do about it. She was very grateful when Mrs Pacific insisted on only taking a short walk. Back at the apartment Antonia left her clothes on a chair and crawled into bed. Tomorrow she would feel better. They were visiting a crocodile park after breakfast. Antonia had never seen crocodiles in real life and couldn't wait.

Someone was shaking Antonia and trying to pull the duvet from her. She clung to it, pulling it over her head.

"Antonia, wake up. Diamond needs us."

Antonia's eyes snapped open as she sat bolt

upright. The room was in semi-darkness and she could just make out Cai standing by the side of her bed. He was dressed in shorts and a T-shirt. With a start, Antonia realised that her silver dolphin charm was thrashing against her neck. Suddenly, it gave out a shrill whistle.

Silver Dolphin, come quickly.

Diamond's voice was hard to hear, as if she was calling from far away.

Diamond, I hear your call, Antonia answered in her head.

She leapt out of bed and reached for her clothes.

"I'll wait outside," said Cai. "Hurry up. I've been trying to wake you for ages."

Antonia pulled on her clothes, wondering why she hadn't heard Diamond's call. As her powers had grown stronger, she had developed telepathy with the dolphins and could sense when she was needed before her charm told her. This sixth sense was even strong enough to wake her when she was sleeping. So why not now?

Uneasily, Antonia picked up her sandals and crept silently from her room. She sat with Cai on the front-door step and they both put on their sandals.

"What time is it?" Antonia whispered.

"Ten to five," Cai whispered back. "Are you ready?"

Antonia nodded and Cai led the way along the road to the flight of steps at the end. They took the steps as fast as was safe in the half-light. The beach stretched before them, vast and empty. Leaving their shoes at the bottom of the steps, Antonia and Cai sprinted to the sea. Antonia breathed deeply, inhaling the fresh salty air as she splashed into the water. It was pleasantly warm and her legs melded together the instant she pushed off from the seabed.

Silver Dolphin, we need you.

Diamond's voice was faint, but there was no mistaking the urgency of her call.

I'm on my way, Antonia answered.

Diamond sounded like she was miles away. Antonia struck out, skimming in and out of the water, anxious to reach her.

Chapter Six

Diamond wasn't as far out at sea as Antonia had expected from the faintness of her call. Her family was there too, but there was no time for friendly greetings. The dolphins had their work cut out supporting a large white bird. Blaze and Swirl were on one side with Diamond, Beauty and Jet on the other.

"It's an albatross," gasped Antonia. Her stomach tightened at the sight of it. One of the bird's wings was stretched out on top of the water while the other was pinned to its side by a very long fishing line that ended in a metal hook cruelly lodged in the bird's curved beak. Its head feathers were rumpled and its dark eyes pleaded for help.

"He got caught in a tuna line," explained Diamond. "Two men were fishing from a boat. When they accidentally snared the bird, they just ditched the line and sailed away."

"How cruel!" Antonia swam to the bird's head, intending to release the hook from its mouth, but as she raised her hand, the bird jerked his head back in panic.

"Steady, boy," crooned Antonia, treading water.

Cai went to free the bird's wing.

"Let me get the hook out first or he might try to fly away," said Antonia.

"Good idea," agreed Cai. "We'll never hold him if he struggles. He's enormous."

Antonia hated seeing such a magnificent creature so vulnerable and bedraggled. Slowly she stretched out her hand. The bird watched with wary eyes, but gradually the panic left him and he relaxed. The fish hook was thicker than the ones Antonia was used to and felt murderously cold to touch. She pushed down on it, but the hook was firmly lodged in the bird's mouth. Blood spurted from the wound on to Antonia's hand as she continued to put pressure on the hook.

The bird's body was tense, but he stayed still, knowing he was being helped. Antonia was conscious of the dolphins watching her and it made her fingers clumsy, but at last the hook came free. Breathing a sigh of relief, she untied it from the twine and stowed it in her pocket.

"Well done," whispered Cai.

The wound needed treatment. Keeping the albatross's beak open, Antonia inserted her fingers back in its mouth.

Heal, she thought.

She imagined the gash knitting together until the bleeding finally stopped.

Heal.

Any minute now Antonia expected to feel a warm glow travel down her hands and into her fingers as the healing magic began to work.

Heal!

Nothing was happening, except for that funny buzzing noise in her head. Trying not to panic, Antonia worked to tune the buzzing out and focus on her healing powers. At last her fingers started to prickle. Excitedly she concentrated on making the albatross better, but to her dismay the prickling sensation faded and the buzzing noise returned. Antonia shook her head, but the noise wouldn't go away.

"Heal!" In desperation she spoke the words aloud.

The bleeding slowed and finally stopped, leaving a nasty wound in the bird's mouth.

"Well done, Silver Dolphin," said Diamond. "I suspected you had higher powers."

"But…" Antonia's voice squeaked with disbelief. "I haven't done anything yet."

"You stopped the bleeding," said Diamond.

"I didn't mend the wound." Antonia was dismayed.

Diamond clicked a short laugh. "Only a very powerful Silver Dolphin can heal wounds completely. You did the best you could. Keep practising and who knows, maybe one day you will have that power too," she said kindly.

Cai's eyes flashed with a mixture of pride and exasperation as he opened his mouth to explain that Antonia could do that already, but Antonia shook her head. She hadn't been able to heal the albatross so what was the point in saying otherwise?

A horrible thought stole through her mind.

Had she overdone things when she'd rescued the turtle? Was it possible to damage her powers, like a sports injury when you pushed yourself too far? The buzzing was still there. It was softer, but as irritating as a trapped fly. Suddenly, Antonia longed to talk to Claudia and ask her about it.

Claudia.

Antonia tried to contact her friend by their special telepathy.

Claudia.

She pictured Claudia's sea-green eyes and her wild, curly brown hair. Where would she be right now? Antonia couldn't remember the time difference between England and Australia except that it was significant.

The buzzing noise in Antonia's head was

still annoying her. It made it hard to think, let alone communicate by telepathy. Frustrated, Antonia gave up then realised that Cai was speaking to her.

"I've loosened the line," he explained. "We'll untie it properly when he's ashore."

"When he's ashore?" Antonia repeated in bewilderment.

"Yes," Cai grinned. "I didn't think you were listening. You had that funny faraway look on your face. Diamond has offered to help us swim the bird to the beach. Then one of us can run up to the apartment and get Mum and Dad to phone for a vet."

"Is everyone coming?" Antonia glanced at the dolphins.

"No," clicked Cai. "We'll be too conspicuous.

Even at this time in the morning there may be people about. Diamond thinks the three of us can manage on our own."

Diamond suggested that Antonia and Cai support the albatross from one side while she took the other. The other dolphins helped while Antonia and Cai swam into position.

"Good luck, Silver Dolphins," clicked Swirl and Jet.

"Good luck," added Blaze and Beauty.

It was awkward swimming the bird back to the beach, but he didn't struggle and Antonia was convinced that he knew he was being helped. Diamond swam as far inshore as she dared without becoming grounded.

"Good luck, Silver Dolphins," she whistled. "I hope you save him."

Antonia and Cai swam on until their knees were bumping on the seabed. As they rose from the sea, the water cascaded from them. Antonia wriggled her toes in the hard, wet sand, marvelling at how one moment her legs felt joined together and the next they were working independently. The albatross felt much heavier once they were out of the water.

"How are we going to do this?" Antonia wondered.

"We won't carry him far," said Cai. "Let's get him a bit further up the beach then one of us can go and get help."

She and Cai rested the bird in the shallow water then, by holding hands, they made a human stretcher to carry him. As Antonia walked slowly up the beach, she reckoned the

albatross weighed almost as much as she did. His wings looked far longer than her arms and he had massive webbed feet.

"Not much further," panted Cai.

The sky was getting lighter. They carried the bird clear of the water and set him down on the golden sand.

"Lucky it's so early," wheezed Antonia, her cheeks red with exertion. "Or we would have had to carry him to those trees to shelter him from the sun."

"We might still have to," said Cai. "It depends how fast the vet can get here. Shall I fetch my parents?"

"Yes," said Antonia, relieved that she didn't have to. Not only was she exhausted, she also felt shy about waking Mr and Mrs Pacific. How would they react to Cai and Antonia being up so early? With a cheery wave, Cai ran off, stopping at the steps to pull on his shoes.

The albatross lay in the sand with his head drooped wearily on his snowy white chest. One black-tipped wing was still tied to his body; the other he had tucked by his side. Antonia checked that the fishing line wasn't hurting him and loosened it in a few more places. She didn't think that the bird would fly away if she freed him completely, but couldn't take that risk. His wound needed treating or he might die from an infection.

As she murmured comforting words, the bird's eyes began to droop. So did Antonia's. She couldn't ever remember feeling this tired before. The faint buzzing in her head had returned. Antonia lay on the sand, pressing her ear to the ground to make the buzzing go away. She didn't mean to fall asleep, but the next thing she knew, Cai was shaking her awake again.

Chapter Seven

"Sleepyhead," Cai teased, but his dark eyes were thoughtful. Embarrassed, Antonia stood up and tried to look alert. Mr and Mrs Pacific were astonished by the sight of the albatross.

"You found it in the shallows?" asked Mrs Pacific for the umpteenth time. "But what were you doing out so early?"

"It's the jet lag," said Cai. "We haven't adjusted to Australian time yet."

Mr Pacific chuckled. "Claudia did warn us that you two had a knack for finding injured animals," he said. "Expect the unexpected were her exact words."

Antonia and Cai shared a smile. Good old Claudia! She must have guessed they would meet up with the local dolphins.

"Did you phone for a vet?" asked Antonia.

"I spoke to the receptionist at the hotel and she told me to ring the North Coast Sea Life Rescue Charity," said Mrs Pacific, running a hand through sleep-tousled hair. "They're used to dealing with this sort of thing. They have a twenty-four-hour emergency helpline. I phoned it and a very friendly lady said she'd send a local officer out. He'll be here shortly."

"That looks like him now," said Cai, pointing to a stocky man coming down the steps to the beach carrying a large bag.

The officer said he had seen far too many albatrosses tangled in fishing line.

"This one's not too bad," he commented, after examining the wound. "It looks like someone's already had a go at treating it."

He glanced up at Antonia and Cai who smiled innocently back.

"Hmmm, well, I'll clean it first then give the bird a shot of antibiotic before we set him free."

The albatross struggled a bit, but the officer was used to birds resisting his help. He worked swiftly and soon the bird was ready to be released.

"Stand back," he warned everyone.

He cut the remaining line away and stepped back himself. The albatross stretched out his enormous wings then tentatively flapped them. Suddenly he was off, running towards the sea, his wings flapping rhythmically. With a stuttering cry, the albatross launched himself in the air and flew away.

"Magic!" sighed Mr Pacific. "What? Why are you laughing?" he added as Antonia and Cai giggled. The officer packed his equipment back into his bag and they walked off the beach together.

Mrs Pacific wanted to go back to bed, but she was outvoted by the others.

"We might as well have an early breakfast and head off to the crocodile park," said her husband.

"It won't be open this time in the morning," grumbled Mrs Pacific as she filled the kettle and began preparing breakfast.

Antonia was feeling better after her short nap on the beach and looking forward to visiting the crocodiles. "I must remember to take my camera," she said. "Jessica will never forgive me if I don't take lots of pictures."

It was fun doing the touristy things, even though the crocodiles' craggy faces and sly, slit-like eyes gave Antonia the creeps. The most exciting part of the day was seeing a real live koala in a tree outside the gift shop. Antonia took several photos before going inside and buying Jessica a cuddly koala that sang 'Waltzing Matilda'.

On the drive home, Antonia reflected that she'd not thought about Silver Dolphins once during the outing. But now her worries came back to her with a bang. Why weren't her higher powers working properly? Was it because of jet lag or was her magic weakening? Antonia shivered, hoping it was the jet lag that was making her feel so bad. She loved being a special Silver Dolphin. Having extra powers, like being able to heal animals, was amazing.

"Have a sweet," said Cai, offering Antonia the crumpled bag he was holding.

Filled with sudden guilt, Antonia blushed. Cai was an ordinary Silver Dolphin. Not once had he moaned or shown any jealousy of Antonia's extra powers. And he'd made a huge difference in their area.

If my powers are fading then I'll manage like Cai, Antonia reassured herself.

But what if your powers go completely? countered a voice in her head.

Antonia pushed the thought away. Of course her powers wouldn't leave her completely. That was a mad idea! Once a Silver Dolphin, always a Silver Dolphin, that's what Claudia had said.

"Sweet?" asked Cai again, jiggling the bag under her nose.

"Thanks." Antonia pulled out a strawberry sherbet and popped it in her mouth, sucking thoughtfully. Whatever happened, she would do her best as a Silver Dolphin.

That evening, the hotel held a barbecue at the restaurant overlooking the beach. Antonia and

Cai joined up with some other children and they had a fun time messing about together.

"I saw a turtle today," boasted a small boy.

"That's nothing – we saw a shark when we were out on my dad's boat," countered another boy.

"My turtle was eating a box jellyfish with massive tentacles. The jellyfish tried to strangle the turtle, but it just sucked the tentacles up like spaghetti."

"My shark was eating a diver," said the second boy. "He ate everything, even the air tanks."

"My mum heard that you rescued an albatross wrapped in a tuna line," said an older girl, pointing at Cai and Antonia. "How cool was that!"

The two boys momentarily stopped arguing and stared at Cai and Antonia.

"An albatross," said one of them in disgust. "That's tame!"

Antonia snorted with laughter, but at the same time the conversation left her feeling slightly uneasy. What if Diamond called upon them to help with a shark or, horror of horrors, a box jellyfish?

Antonia was terrified of all jellyfish, even harmless ones, having suffered a nasty allergic reaction when she'd been stung by one before. Would her powers be enough to deal with such dangerous creatures? Antonia wished she knew what was happening to her, and if there was anything she could do to stop it.

Chapter Eight

"Tag!" clicked Jet, tossing a battered strip of seaweed at Antonia. "You're it! Or shall we stop this game and have a water fight?"

"Water fight," whistled Cai, swimming up behind them. "But first you promised to show me how to breach."

"Is there time?" Antonia asked, half hoping

that Cai would agree there wasn't. They'd been in the sea for ages and she was feeling tired again. It was the day after the crocodile trip and Diamond had called them for another mission. To Antonia's consternation, Cai had heard Diamond's call first.

"The dolphins need us," he'd said, when Antonia didn't respond.

At first Antonia couldn't hear her charm at all. She'd felt it fluttering against her neck and had had to concentrate very hard to hear Diamond's shrill whistle.

Luckily the call hadn't been urgent. The mission had been to clear up some litter thrown overboard from a passing boat. After learning about the blue ringed octopus, Antonia was wary about collecting rubbish.

But she had kept her fears to herself and worked hard to pick it all up. With or without her special powers, she was determined to be a good Silver Dolphin.

"The carrier bags are the worst," Diamond had said, her silver body shivering in disgust as one floated by. "Turtles mistake them for jellyfish then suffocate when eating them."

Antonia and Cai had recovered three carrier bags and filled them with the rest of the rubbish. Diamond told them to leave the bags on a nearby beach while they played with Jet and Swirl.

"You deserve a treat. We've been working you hard," she had clicked.

Antonia and Cai didn't need rewards for being Silver Dolphins, but were thrilled to play with their new friends again. First they had swum the rubbish to the secluded bay and left it on the beach where they'd rescued the turtle.

"We'll come back for it later," Cai had said, wedging the bags between some rocks.

Jet and Swirl had waited for them out at sea; Jet with a long strip of seaweed on his nose ready to play seaweed tag.

They played for ages until Cai asked to be taught how to breach. Jet helped Cai while Swirl helped Antonia.

"Wicked!" exclaimed Cai, when he'd finally got the move. "I can't wait to show Bubbles and get him back for all the times he's splashed me."

Jet and Cai joined forces against Swirl and

Antonia and between them they churned the sea into a frothy whirlpool. It was such fun splashing each other and Antonia was annoyed when she tired before everyone else and let the boys get the better of her team.

"Enough," she panted. "We ought to go before your mum and dad miss us."

Cai reluctantly agreed.

"Next time we'll beat the boys," Swirl clicked in Antonia's ear before they left. Antonia had to concentrate really hard to understand what Swirl was saying. Her voice sounded like it was coming from far away. It didn't help that the buzzing noise was back in her head and that it was so loud it made her feel dizzy.

Antonia suddenly felt exhausted and longed

to be back on land. She wasn't sure she had the energy to tow the rubbish home and was grateful when Cai insisted that he collect the bags from the beach on his own.

"It doesn't need both of us," he assured Antonia.

Antonia pushed her wet hair away from her face. She and Cai usually did everything together, no matter how small the task. Had Cai guessed she was tired again? He didn't mention it, but when he returned with the carrier bags, he only let Antonia take one from him.

"Thanks," she said gratefully.

"I should be thanking you. It's easier to swim with two bags," Cai said as they swam back to the hotel beach.

The rest of the day was spent lazing around

one of the hotel pools with Cai's parents. Antonia stayed in the shallow end, lazily floating in the cool water while Cai and his mum and dad had swimming races and then a noisy water fight. Antonia knew she wasn't being very good company, but Cai was having so much fun he didn't seem to notice.

Bedtime couldn't come soon enough and at last Antonia was able to go to her room. She was incredibly tired, but no sooner had she laid down her head than it filled with worrying thoughts. *What was that buzzing noise? Was it because the Silver Dolphin magic wasn't working properly? What if it failed her completely?*

Antonia choked back a sob. She couldn't bear it if she wasn't a Silver Dolphin any more. Her fingers strayed to her silver dolphin charm. It lay on her neck, reassuringly soft as always.

There, you're being silly, she scolded herself. Her magic must be working or the charm would feel hard and cold like real silver. Antonia tried to chase all the unpleasant thoughts away by thinking about Bubbles and Dream. She wondered if they were missing her as much as she was missing them.

Restlessly, Antonia tossed and turned. The air conditioning was making her throat dry. It was still very warm outside, but Antonia longed to open a window and let the night air in. It was a long time before she drifted into a troubled sleep. Then a short while later she woke with a terrible pain in her head. She clutched at it with her hands. Her face was burning and her whole body ached.

"Oooooh," she moaned.

She felt awful. Tears prickled under her eyelids then rolled down her face. There was only one thing Antonia wanted now and it was something she couldn't have. Antonia wanted her mum.

Chapter Nine

Cai was woken up by Antonia moaning and came to see if she was all right.

"I'll go and get Mum," he said the moment he saw her.

After that everything was a blur. Antonia was conscious of Mrs Pacific talking in a low, soothing voice then someone laying

a damp flannel on her forehead. Ages later a lady with flowery perfume and a strong Australian accent came and sat on the edge of her bed.

"I'm Doctor Melanie Collard," she said. "Can you tell me where it hurts?"

"My head," moaned Antonia.

Gently, the doctor helped Antonia upright so she could examine her. She looked down her throat and shone a light into her ears.

"Woah!" she exclaimed. "That's some ear infection you've got. No wonder your head hurts. Has it been like it for long?"

"Yes," croaked Antonia. "It's been buzzing for days."

"I'm not surprised. You'll need a strong antibiotic for that. The pharmacy in town won't be open until the morning, but in the meantime I'll give you something for the pain."

Antonia closed her eyes as Dr Collard rustled in her bag. She felt something cold on her skin then a sharp prick.

"That should help," said the doctor kindly. "Now try and get some sleep."

Gratefully, Antonia drifted off. She slept fitfully, waking every now and then, and each time the room was lighter. Much later she was aware of people quietly moving around the apartment. Antonia stayed where she was, not well enough to get up. Then Mrs Pacific came in and asked if she wanted anything to eat. Antonia shook her head, but allowed Mrs Pacific to help her sit up to take a sip from a glass of iced water. She wiped her mouth with

the back of her hand then wearily sank back on to the pillows.

"Lenny and Cai have run into town to get your prescription," said Mrs Pacific. "I'll phone your mum later and tell her you're not well. You can speak to her too. They're about nine hours behind us so I won't ring yet. We don't want to frighten your mum by ringing in the middle of the night."

Antonia gave Mrs Pacific a weak grin. Although she badly wanted to see her mum right then, she didn't feel up to talking to her on the phone. Hopefully, she would later. Mrs Pacific chattered on as she plumped Antonia's pillows and straightened her bed.

"You're to take it easy while the antibiotics start to work. No swimming – doctor's orders!

Though I don't suppose you'll want to swim anyway. Shall I draw the curtains? No? Do you want the television on then?"

"No thanks." Antonia's head wasn't hurting as badly as it had in the night, but it was still very sore and the buzzing in her ear was making it hard to concentrate. She lay on her back, staring up at the ceiling, trying to make sense of her jumbled thoughts.

When Cai and his dad returned, they came in to visit Antonia. With a wide grin, Mr Pacific held out grapes and a bouquet of exotic-looking flowers.

"For the patient," he said grandly.

Antonia swallowed back the lump in her throat. No wonder Cai was kind; his parents were so thoughtful.

"Cai, no!" Mr Pacific playfully smacked Cai's hand as he reached out for a grape.

"That's all right," said Antonia. "It's a huge bunch. There's plenty to share."

"You have to take one of these as well." Mr Pacific pulled out a box from his pocket and then snapped a tablet from the foil-covered sheet inside.

"Crikey!" he exclaimed. "Do you think the doctor ordered the right thing? It's enormous. Looks like the kind of tablet you'd give a horse."

With a cheeky grin, he read the label on the box. "It's definitely got your name on it. Better take a large swig of water then."

Antonia wasn't keen on taking tablets and was concentrating on drinking enough water to swallow it, so at first she didn't notice

Cai's agitation. It wasn't until he started hopping up and down that she realised something was wrong.

"Erm, I was wondering if..." Cai's face was red with embarrassment as he struggled to find the right words.

Suddenly Antonia noticed the silver dolphin charm pinned to his T-shirt. It was vibrating. Her hand flew to her own necklace and the dolphin's tail fluttered against her fingers like a feather in the wind. Only a Silver Dolphin could see and hear when the dolphins were calling. Mr Pacific didn't notice a thing and smiled encouragingly at Cai while he waited for him to finish his sentence. Antonia was aware of a clicking noise and fought the buzzing in her head to listen to it.

Diamond, I hear your call, she silently clicked back.

But could she answer the call when she felt so ill?

"You're not allowed to go swimming, are you?" said Cai, guessing her line of thought.

"No, but..."

"No buts!" said Mr Pacific heartily. "Definitely no swimming."

"No, but Cai can go if he wants to," said Antonia in a rush. "Don't hang around here for me. I might get up soon and read or something." She hoped she sounded convincing. She minded dreadfully that Cai would answer Diamond's call without her!

"Well, if you're sure." Cai was already at the door.

"Cai!" Mr Pacific was shocked.

"I'm cool with it. Really, Mr Pacific," said Antonia. "It's not Cai's fault I've got an ear infection. I'd hate him to stay in just for me."

"Go on then, hop it," Mr Pacific sighed.

"Thanks," said Cai, disappearing at a run.

"I'm going to read for a bit." Antonia had no intention of reading, but hoped Mr Pacific would get the hint and leave.

This was awful. She hated not being able to hear Diamond properly and she hated not being able to answer the call. Would Cai be all right on his own? The Australian ocean was very different from the English one. Images of sharks, box jellyfish and blue ringed octopus – all things Cai might

encounter when answering Diamond's call – flashed through her mind. Petrified, Antonia lay in bed waiting for Cai to return. Surely his Silver Dolphin magic would keep him safe, wouldn't it?

Chapter Ten

"It was fine," said Cai. "At first I was terrified I'd meet a shark, but once I was in the water I forgot all about that. The task wasn't difficult. One of Diamond's pod, a dolphin called Streak, had cut his fin on a broken bottle. I blotted it with seaweed until the bleeding stopped, then I collected up the

glass and brought it ashore. If only everyone thought to take their rubbish home with them, the sea would be a much safer place."

"Did you tell Diamond about me being ill?"

"Yes, she was very interested. She thought that Spirit had exaggerated your powers. She thinks your magic will be stronger when you're feeling better."

Antonia breathed a sigh of relief. She'd come to the same conclusion herself, that her loss of power was due to her ear infection, but it was nice to have it confirmed.

"So Diamond's spoken to Spirit. How did that happen?"

"They met, halfway between here and Australia. Remember Spirit went away a couple of days before we left home? Well, that's where he was. He used dolphin magic to contact Diamond. She was only too glad to meet up with Spirit when she heard about us."

"That's great," said Antonia. "Did you play with the dolphins?"

"For a bit." Cai looked sheepish. "Jet and Swirl asked and I couldn't let them down, could I?"

"Of course not," Antonia agreed. "I feel such a lazy lump being stuck in bed."

"You are," said Cai, laughing.

"Your mum won't let me get up!" Antonia was indignant.

"Quite right too. You look awful."

"I feel it." Antonia hated admitting that. She wanted everything back to normal. Being ill was no fun and she couldn't help feeling

envious of Cai who'd answered a call on his own and got to play with the dolphins.

Even with the antibiotics it took Antonia longer than she'd hoped to recover. She spent the rest of the day in bed and the following day, feeling only a little better, Mrs Pacific made her a bed on the sofa in the lounge. Mrs Pacific was very kind, fussing over her and keeping her supplied with cold drinks and a stack of DVDs to watch, but Antonia badly missed her own mum. It was good to speak to her on the telephone and she'd spoken with her dad and Jessica too.

On the third day following the doctor's visit Antonia felt well enough to get dressed. Mr Pacific put the sun umbrella up and she sat on the patio reading and occasionally watching the sea. Cai wanted to keep her company, but Antonia was happy to be on left on her own, insisting that Cai spend time with each of his parents. She felt awful that they couldn't go out as a family because someone had to stay behind and look after her.

"It's no problem," Mrs Pacific assured her. "You'll have to visit us again. You've missed out too."

"I'm surprised you'd want me back after the trouble I've caused."

Mrs Pacific laughed. "You're worth it," she said kindly. "I'm so relieved Cai has you for a friend. Lenny and I worry about leaving him in England, but now I've met you I can see we don't need to."

To her frustration, Antonia felt very weak after

her first day out of bed and decided on an early night. She was going to read, but fell asleep immediately and dreamt she was swimming alone at night in the ocean. The dream was scary; in it she was battling with a box jellyfish. Its long tentacles snagged round her legs as its soft jelly body smothered her face.

Antonia woke with a pounding heart to find her reading book over her nose and the duvet twisted tightly round her legs. It took a little while for her heart to slow and even longer to free herself from the duvet. At last Antonia was able to reach for the bedside light and switch it on.

She lay propped against her pillows, staring at the picture of the leaping dolphins. *What would Spirit and Diamond and their pods be doing now?*

Thinking about her dolphins made Antonia's eyes feel weary again. She snuggled down in bed, but as she began to doze, something tickled her neck. Sleepily, she brushed it with her hand. The tickle grew stronger and a soft clicking noise filled the room.

Antonia jerked awake, her fingers reaching for her silver dolphin necklace. It was vibrating. Faster and faster the vibrations grew until the dolphin's soft body was thrumming against her neck like raindrops on a window. A shrill whistle echoed round the room.

Hurry, Silver Dolphin.

Diamond, I hear your call.

In a flash Antonia was out of bed and pulling her clothes from the wardrobe. "Ooh!" she exclaimed, clutching at the wardrobe door.

She'd moved too fast and now her head was spinning. She stood quietly for a moment while her body recovered. The dolphin charm beat wildly against her skin.

Diamond, I'm on my way.

Antonia pulled her clothes on over the top of her pyjamas then, hearing footsteps outside her room, tiptoed to the door and peeped out. Cai was creeping down the hallway.

"Wait!" whispered Antonia.

"Antonia! You scared the life out of me."

In the moonlight shining into the hall Cai's face was unusually pale. "Go back to bed. I can manage on my own."

"But it's the middle of the night," whispered Antonia.

"So?"

"It'll be safer if there are two of us."

"The dolphin magic will keep me safe. The doctor said no swimming."

"Yes, but my ear's fine now," Antonia lied. "I'm coming with you."

"You're not!" Cai folded his arms and glared at her.

Antonia glared back with a mixture of emotions filling her head. How dare Cai insist he went off on his own? He couldn't tell her what to do. She was a Silver Dolphin too.

"Please, Antonia?"

Antonia's anger evaporated. Cai wasn't trying to be bossy or mean. He was just concerned. "Look, I wouldn't lie to you. I'm fine. I want to come. Let's not waste time arguing. This call feels urgent."

Cai grinned. "Antonia Lee, you *are* lying," he insisted. "Please go back to bed or I'll be forced to wake Mum and Dad."

"You wouldn't!" Antonia was shocked. "Then neither of us could answer the call."

Cai said nothing and Antonia couldn't make up her mind if he was bluffing or not. The seconds ticked by until a loud, urgent whistle filled the hall.

Silver Dolphin, COME QUICKLY!

Antonia knew she was beaten. "All right," she said with a sigh. "I won't come. But I'm not going back to bed. I'm waiting on the patio until you get back."

Cai reached out and, brushing her on the arm, whispered, "Thanks." Swiftly, he opened the front door and disappeared into the dark.

Chapter Eleven

ollecting a jumper from her room and wrapping it around her shoulders, Antonia softly opened the lounge doors and went and stood on the patio. After a while she saw a dark shape running across the beach. Even though she knew Cai wouldn't see her, she leant over the balcony and waved. Without

hesitation Cai splashed into the water and swam away.

Antonia experienced a sudden pang of unease. Had she been right to let him go off on his own? Spirit had warned her a long time ago that being a Silver Dolphin could be dangerous.

The waiting was awful. At first Antonia sat curled in a ball on a sun lounger, but she was too restless to be still for long and hung over the balcony, her eyes searching for signs of life in the sea. Where was Cai now and what was he doing? Did Claudia feel the same anxiety and helplessness when Antonia and Cai answered the call, leaving her behind?

Lit by a huge round moon, the sea stretched away, a black cloak rippling in the breeze.

Antonia touched her necklace for reassurance. The charm had stopped vibrating, but every now and then she felt it quiver as if it was trying to tell her something. Antonia closed her eyes and cleared a space in her head. It was easier to concentrate now the buzzing had gone. Soon the space was filled with a whisper. The whisper grew louder and more insistent.

Come quickly, Silver Dolphin, we need you.

Antonia knew this second call was meant for her. Straightaway she answered.

Diamond, I hear your call.

Swiftly and quietly, she went back inside, locking the patio doors, then creeping through the sleeping house to go back out through the front door. She ran down the deserted road, hesitating at the steps, before hurtling down

them as fast as was safe. At the bottom she stumbled, tripping over Cai's abandoned shoes.

"Ouch!" Antonia mumbled a curse as she threw her sandals next to Cai's, then hared across the beach with only the moon to light her way. As she paddled into the sea, Antonia realised that neither she nor Cai had left a note for his parents. Crossing her fingers, she willed them not to wake up until morning.

The sea was chillier than she'd been expecting. Teeth chattering noisily, Antonia waded further into the water. She didn't start swimming until she was in up to her waist. At first the coldness made her wince, but as her legs melded together and her body took on dolphin-like characteristics, she soon forgot the cold. Using her hands for flippers and kicking her legs together like a tail, Antonia swam in the dark ocean.

It was fantastic being in the water again after so many days moping around in bed. Antonia's muscles tingled with exhilaration as she leapt in and out of the sea. This was better than flying! The magic propelled Antonia along faster than a real dolphin as she raced to answer Diamond's call.

Even with the moon's light it wasn't easy to work out exactly where she was, but Antonia thought she was travelling parallel to the hotel beach. Sensing vibrations to her left, she turned towards the coastline. The hotel was as clear to see as a patch of daylight, lights blazing from every angle. Antonia slowed, seeing and sensing dark shapes in the water ahead.

"Silver Dolphin, you came."

Diamond broke away from the group of dolphins anxiously milling around and rubbed noses with her in greeting.

"I'm sorry I didn't come more quickly." Antonia's face was hot with embarrassment.

"I wouldn't have called if it wasn't so urgent," clicked Diamond. "I know you're not completely better. Are you sure you're able to help?"

"Yes," Antonia nodded emphatically. "Tell me what to do."

"You're needed on the beach." Diamond nodded her head in the direction of the shore where Antonia could just make out a small cove. She screwed up her eyes, trying to work out where she was. Then she got it. It was the secluded cove round the corner from the hotel's private beach where they'd rescued the turtle. That incident seemed such a long time ago, it was no wonder Antonia hadn't recognised where she was.

Cai was on the beach, dashing about the sand like a battery-operated toy. But what was he doing? Antonia trod water, fascinated by his antics. One minute Cai would stoop down then the next he ran over to squat at the edge of the sea.

"What's happened?" Antonia asked Diamond.

The dolphin took a deep breath, her eyes glinting in the moonlight as she explained. "For years this beach has been a nesting place for turtles. The turtle is an amazing creature. It returns to the beach where it was born to mate, sometimes swimming thousands of miles to get there. The female turtle comes ashore and buries her eggs in the sand. Then she swims away, leaving the eggs incubating until the baby turtles are ready to hatch.

"This happens at night when, drawn by the light of the moon, the tiny turtles dash to the sea to avoid being eaten by crabs, lizards and birds. But the artificial lights of the beachside developments confuse the hatchlings. Instead of crawling towards the sea, the baby turtles are drawn up the beach towards the settlements. They become stranded inland where they're an easy catch for predators.

"Tonight baby turtles are hatching on the beach, but the lights from the new hotel are confusing them. Help them, Silver Dolphin. Help them to find the right way down to the sea."

Antonia was dismayed. She was staying at that hotel and it made her feel responsible for the plight of the turtles. But feeling guilty wasn't going to help them. Action was needed. Antonia swam to the beach, but as she waded ashore, the enormity of the task almost swamped her. The beach was covered with hundreds of tiny turtles. How could she and Cai possibly help them all?

Chapter Twelve

Antonia stood helplessly watching the hundreds of hatchling turtles scrambling the wrong way up the beach until Cai ran up beside her.

"Are you OK? Do you need to sit down?"

"I'm fine."

Cai's concern snapped Antonia out of her

trance. There was no point letting the task overwhelm her; she had better get on with it.

"Start with the ones higher up the beach," instructed Cai. "They're in the most danger. I've already chased a goanna into the trees."

Antonia shuddered, not wanting to think about the enormous lizard snacking on baby turtles. With a determined frown, she ran up the beach, the hard, wet sand turning soft and powdery the further she went. There were turtles everywhere and she had to watch where she was treading. As she came closer to the trees, the number of turtles began to thin, but they were all still travelling in the wrong direction.

Stooping down, Antonia plucked two baby turtles from the beach. There was no time to wonder at how cute they were. Antonia carried the turtles down to the sea, ignoring the tickling sensation of their tiny flippers as they fought to climb out of her cupped hands. Carefully, she eased the turtles on to the sand and waited until they'd pulled themselves into the surf. Then it was another dash back up the beach to rescue more.

The job was endless: run, bend, scoop, run, bend, put the turtles by the sea and start again. Before long Antonia's legs were aching and her breathing heavy. She stopped for a moment to recover and, pushing her long blonde hair over her shoulders, stared up at the moon. It was hopeless! They would never be able to rescue even a fraction of the turtles at this rate.

Cai came and stood next to her, a turtle in

each hand. "We can do this," he urged.

"But we can't," said Antonia simply. "There are too many turtles to save them all. We need help."

"I could go and get Mum and Dad." Cai sounded doubtful.

Antonia smiled at him, but they both knew it wasn't practical.

"Torches," said Cai. "What if we got powerful torches and shone them up the beach? The turtles would head towards the light thinking it was the moon."

"Where are we going to get powerful torches at this time of night?" Antonia said, hating to sound so negative.

Cai shrugged. "It was just a thought."

"And a good one, but it's not like we've got

Claudia and Sea Watch to call on. We don't know anyone like that here."

Cai sighed. "Better get back to it then and do what we can. Maybe a miracle will happen or something."

"I'll start wishing for that miracle," said Antonia lightly.

They worked in silence, the only noise coming from their feet scrunching in the sand and the soft swoosh of the surf as it washed ashore. Once Antonia accidentally kicked a tiny turtle, sending it spinning on to its back so its flippers waved helplessly in the air. She dropped to her knees and plucked it from the sand.

"I'm sorry," she whispered. "I didn't mean to hurt you."

Carefully, she took the turtle down the beach

and put it in the sea. The moment the surf tickled its flipper-like legs the turtle swam away, kicking for all it was worth. Longingly, Antonia watched it go. She had a sudden, desperate urge to follow the turtle. The urge was so strong it reminded her of the first time she'd worn her silver dolphin necklace. She'd been drawn to the sea and, following her impulse, had been led to Spirit and his dolphins.

Cai came up, giving her a furtive sidelong look as he released two more turtles into the sea.

"Sorry, I'm slacking again." Antonia hurried back up the beach for more hatchlings.

The birds came from nowhere. One minute Antonia and Cai were alone with the turtles and the next they were being bombarded by

seabirds. Like a military campaign the birds dived, plucking the tiny turtles from the beach and carrying them away for a late-night meal.

"Shoo, go away!" Antonia and Cai abandoned their rescue mission to chase the birds, but there were too many of them to protect every turtle.

Antonia glared at the brightly lit hotel complex. This was such a beautiful spot. Why did the harsh artificial lighting have to outshine the beauty of the moon? If it wasn't there then the turtles would be safe. They had to save them, but how?

Antonia's brain worked so hard to find a solution, it made her head ache. Filled with longing, she turned to face the sea. She desperately wanted to be back in the moonlit water. Without realising what she was doing, Antonia walked towards the surf.

"Wait!" cried Cai. "Where are you going?"

"Come with me."

It was like being in a dream; Antonia had little control over herself. All she knew was that she had a powerful urge to get into the water. Cai chased after her and caught her by the hand.

"Antonia, what is it? Are you all right?"

"Yes." Antonia clutched at Cai with strength she didn't know she had, pulling him along with her. An idea was stirring in her mind. It was huge and she didn't know if she could achieve it. But as the idea grew, so did Antonia's new strength and she knew she must try.

Chapter Thirteen

The water was so refreshing it woke Antonia from her dazed state. The enormity of what she was about to do hit her. If she pulled this off, it would be the incredible miracle she'd wished for. If she failed then at least she'd given it her all.

The water was up to her thighs when she

dived, swimming with powerful, dolphin-like strokes as her legs melded together. She could feel Diamond and the other dolphins watching her. As she drew closer, a whispering noise sounded inside her head.

Silver Dolphin, you can do this.

Antonia glanced up, her eyes searching for Diamond.

Thank you, she answered.

Cai splashed behind her in the moonlit water. Antonia swam on, conscious that Diamond's whole pod had turned out. It was much bigger than Spirit's; Antonia guessed there were at least fifty dolphins all silently supporting her. She swam through the dolphins and into a clear patch of ocean. Then, neatly flipping on to her back, she floated in

the water and stared at the vast night sky. She was vaguely aware that Cai had stopped a short distance away, treading water while he waited for her next move.

Antonia cast her mind back to the day they'd rescued the turtle from the fishing net. Like now, the task had almost been too big, the stones insignificant against the thick rope. By accident, she'd pushed her powers further than ever before, magically helping the stone to cut the rope and free the turtle. Was it possible to use that power again, this time to strengthen the light of the moon? Taking a deep breath, Antonia locked her eyes on the silvery ball hanging in the sky.

Brighten.

She stared up, her concentration unwavering.

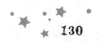

Moon, brighten.

A warm feeling that started in Antonia's heart slowly spread through the rest of her body. It made her fingers and limbs tingle until her whole body felt like it was glowing. Antonia imagined reaching out to the moon and touching it with her fingertips. She continued to stare skywards. The moon seemed much larger, as if it was coming closer. Was it really shining more brightly?

It was exhausting work. Antonia couldn't help a small lapse in her concentration and all at once the moon started slipping away, growing smaller and paler.

Brighten!

Antonia rallied herself, refusing to give in to her tired body. For the sake of the turtles she could do this. She lay in the water, willing the moon to outshine the hotel lights that threatened the turtles' survival. Suddenly, Antonia was aware of a circle of dolphins forming around her. With soft clicks they swam closer together and soon it was impossible to tell where one dolphin ended and the next began. Their presence was uplifting.

Antonia felt her magic surge. She directed it at the moon, hurling it upwards. The moon caught the magic and shone it back with such brightness that it lit the sea for miles around. Faster and faster the dolphins swam and now they were singing, their beautiful voices ringing out with joy.

But was it enough? Would the moon's light draw the turtles away from the land and into the sea? Antonia had her answer as hundreds of tiny hatchling turtles swam past her, all hurrying away to start their new lives.

We did it! Antonia thought the words in her head, not daring to say them out loud in case it broke the magic.

I'm so proud of you, Silver Dolphin.

Antonia went ice-cold with shock.

Claudia?

Well done.

Claudia's voice kept breaking up like she was speaking on a mobile phone when the signal was bad.

See you soon, Silver Dolphin.

You too.

At last Antonia felt able to relax. She lay on her back, floating in the middle of the

circle of dolphins, watching the turtles swim past, the occasional one bumping into her. A long while later, when the turtles had finally petered out, the dolphins stopped circling and one by one broke away. Reluctantly, Antonia righted herself.

Cai swam over and there was no need for words. Cai's face, a reflection of her own, said everything. Antonia reached out and, in the way of the dolphins, triumphantly greeted him nose to nose.

Chapter Fourteen

Now it was over Antonia was exhausted and wasn't sure if she had enough energy to swim home. Diamond's pod all wanted to thank the Silver Dolphins and milled around, brushing them with their flippers until Diamond spoke. "The Silver Dolphins look tired. Who will help them to swim home?"

The whole pod volunteered for the job and Diamond chose half of them, including Jet and Swirl. Soon Antonia and Cai were each surrounded by a group of dolphins. They floated on their backs, letting the dolphins push them home. It was the most wonderful ride Antonia had ever had and she was truly sorry when it was over.

"Thanks, everyone," she clicked. "Seaweed tag next time?" she added to Jet and Swirl.

"Bubbly," they clicked back.

Antonia whistled a laugh. "You sound just like Bubbles. He's my friend back home."

Usually, after answering a call, Antonia and Cai watched the dolphins swim out to sea, but this time the dolphins watched them swim ashore. There was lots of nose rubbing and slapping of flippers against hands to say goodbye before they went. Tired as she was, Antonia said an extra special goodbye to Jet and Swirl, rubbing noses with her new friends and stroking their fins.

"See you soon, Silver Dolphins," whistled Jet and Swirl.

"Yes," said Antonia, sensing that it wouldn't be long before she saw the dolphins again.

She was grateful when the water was shallow enough to put her feet down. The moment Antonia stood up, her legs stopped feeling joined like a tail and began to work independently. Water poured from her clothes and splashed on to the sand leaving her completely dry. She padded up the beach with Cai and by the time they reached their shoes,

only their slightly damp hair gave away their night-swimming activities.

The flight of steps back to the apartment seemed to go on forever. Cai held Antonia up by the arm as she struggled up it, concentrating on one step at a time, not daring to check how far she had to go. At last she reached the top.

"That was amazing," said Cai, stopping to catch his breath. "You did a great job out there. If it wasn't for you, most of those turtles would have died."

"We both did a great job," said Antonia firmly.

They walked up the road in silence. Cai looked relaxed and happy; however, something was niggling at Antonia. She couldn't put her finger on why the job didn't feel finished. She was sure there was something more to do, but no matter how hard she racked her brains she couldn't think what.

They had almost reached their holiday apartment when Cai hesitated. "Did you leave a light on?" he asked. Antonia shook her head.

"Well, there's one on now." Cai caught his breath. "And someone's at the front door."

"It's your dad," groaned Antonia. "Now we're for It."

Mr Pacific stepped outside, quietly pulling the door shut. "What's going on?" he whispered.

"It's my fault," said Cai and Antonia together. A faint smile crossed Mr Pacific's face.

"Antonia couldn't sleep," said Cai quickly. "That happens when you've been ill, doesn't

it? You spend so much time in bed that when you start to feel better, you can't sleep at night. Anyway, I saw her light on after I got up to use the toilet, so I went in. She was wide awake and I thought a walk might help her get to sleep again. We didn't go far, just to the end of the road and back."

Mr Pacific said nothing and Antonia held her breath, hoping he hadn't noticed their damp hair. Eventually he said, "That probably wasn't one of your smartest ideas, Cai. You're lucky Mum didn't wake and find you gone. She'd have the whole of the Australian police force mobilised by now."

"Sorry," said Cai meekly.

"Me too," Antonia added.

"Never mind," said Mr Pacific.

Before they went back to bed, Mr Pacific made Antonia and Cai a mug of hot chocolate.

"That'll help you sleep," he said, setting the steaming mugs down on the table.

Antonia was so tired it took all her strength not to fall asleep in her drink! She sipped it as fast as she could then thankfully crawled into bed.

Both Cai and Antonia slept late and woke to the smell of scrambled eggs. Dressing quickly, Antonia found Mrs Pacific preparing an extravagant breakfast of scrambled eggs, toast, smoked salmon and strawberries. They ate on the patio and halfway through breakfast Antonia suddenly realised what had been bugging her last night. She almost choked on a piece of toast. When she'd stopped coughing,

Mrs Pacific topped up her glass from a jug on the table.

"Have a drink. I hope you're not getting a cold on top of the ear infection. Perhaps you ought to have another day indoors?"

Antonia was alarmed. She couldn't stay in. There was an important job to do. "I'm fine, really I am. A piece of toast went down the wrong way. Cai and I had arranged to go for a walk this morning. If that's all right?"

Cai nearly fell off his chair in surprise.

"It's a great idea." Mrs Pacific smiled. "But remember to take it easy. You'll need time to build up your strength. Tomorrow I thought we'd visit the Lost City. It's an amazing place. Incredible sandstone towers in a National Park setting. The waterfalls are supposed to be stunning."

"Great!" said Antonia and Cai enthusiastically.

Mrs Pacific reached for the newspaper. "If you're both finished, you might as well go on that walk. You look itching to get started."

"Thanks, Mrs Pacific." Antonia jumped up. "Come on, Cai."

Chapter Fifteen

In her bedroom Antonia hastily applied suncream, put on her hat and found her camera. Cai was waiting for her by the front door with a couple of bottles of water.

"Mum gave us these. She said not to walk too far in the heat." He lowered his voice. "So where are we going?"

"To the turtle beach," Antonia whispered back.

"Why?" asked Cai. "Did you leave something behind?"

Putting her finger to her lips, Antonia gestured for Cai to follow her outside where they couldn't be overheard.

"The turtles are still in danger," she said. "I remembered that turtles lay more than one lot of eggs in a season. We may have saved this batch of hatchlings, but what about the next ones?"

Cai's eyes widened. "You're right!" he exclaimed. "I read that somewhere too. But what can we do about it? We won't be here when the next lot of turtles hatch."

"Well," said Antonia slowly. "I was thinking

that if we could prove the beach is a nesting site for turtles, we might be able to persuade the hotel to do something about its lights."

"It's worth a try," said Cai. "Do you know how to get to the beach? We've only ever swum there before."

"It's on the other side of the hotel. I thought we'd walk that way and see what happens."

In companionable silence they walked round the hotel, past the car park and on through the hotel's carefully maintained grounds. After a while the plants became wilder and the footpath petered out. Antonia and Cai soon found themselves scrambling over rocks.

"Watch where you're putting your feet and make lots of noise," said Cai, stomping noisily.

"Why?"

"In case there are snakes." Cai laughed at her horrified reaction. "Don't worry. You won't get bitten if you're careful."

Soon they came across a familiar belt of trees. "We're here," said Antonia, grinning in delight.

They wove their way on to the beach. Antonia screwed up her eyes at the dazzling sun. "There!" she said triumphantly. "Look at the sand. Does that say turtles or not?"

"Turtles," agreed Cai. They stared at the markings covering the beach. "This one's like a wiggly tyre track," he continued.

"That'll be an adult," said Antonia, squatting down to take photographs. "The marks are too big to have been made by the hatchlings. Oh, look, Cai, a piece of eggshell!"

Antonia snapped away with her camera,

collecting as much evidence of the turtles as she could. Sadly, she found a couple of dead hatchlings, although not much was left of them.

"I've been thinking," said Cai. "It might be better to pass this on to a conservation charity. They'll know exactly what to do. They might even get the hotel to work with them. They could make the beach a tourist attraction. I'm sure people go on turtle-watching holidays."

"That's a brilliant idea." Antonia's eyes shone with excitement. "Let's ring the North Coast Sea Life Rescue Charity. I bet they'd help."

Kicking off her sandals, she sank down on the warm sand while she put her camera away in its bag.

"I've taken loads of photos and we can take some shell back too..."

Antonia broke off as a funny sensation swept over her. Her heart soared. Her ear was clearly on the mend! Sensing that Diamond was about to call, Antonia lightly brushed her silver dolphin charm and was rewarded by a small flutter of its tail. A minute later the dolphin charm began to vibrate and click.

Silver Dolphin, we need you.

Diamond, I hear your call.

Jumping up, Antonia ran and hid her camera, water bottle and shoes under a tree before racing back down the beach.

"Antonia… oh!" Cai's hand flew to the silver dolphin charm pinned to his T-shirt then, with a wide smile, hurried after her.

Side by side they splashed into the warm water. Antonia sensed the call wasn't urgent, but was eager to meet up with the dolphins. The moment her legs melded together she swam, dipping in and out of the water, loving the feeling of flying as she raced through the sea. Cai swam beside her, his body arching like a real dolphin.

When they were a fair way out, they spotted Diamond with two smaller dolphins hovering by her side. Jet and Swirl! Antonia wanted to swim straight to their friends, but remembering her role as a Silver Dolphin, she approached Diamond first.

"Thank you for answering the call, Silver Dolphins." Diamond greeted Antonia and Cai with a friendly rub on the nose, then waited while they said hello to Jet and Swirl.

"It's not urgent this time. Jet and Swirl found

some litter that needs clearing up. They've offered to show you where."

"This way, Silver Dolphins," clicked Jet.

He dived underwater with Swirl, Antonia and Cai following close behind. Beneath her Antonia could see a dark shadow and as she drew closer she caught her breath.

"It's beautiful!"

The coral reef stretching beneath them was the most wondrous thing Antonia had ever seen. Thick with corals of every shape and size, the reef was as colourful as a carnival float and came in every shade of the rainbow from pastel pink to vibrant blue. Fish flitted around – striped, spotted and some with long feathery tails – while beautiful red tube worms waved their fan-shaped plumes.

"Over here," clicked Jet, diving towards a rock with squiggly marks that made it look like a brain. Suspiciously, Antonia and Cai swam closer to a yellow and black object that looked out of place on the reef.

"It's a diver's torch!" exclaimed Cai, reaching out for it. Anxiously, Antonia looked about. "Do you think someone's still down here? What if they see us?"

"It's broken." Cai flicked at the switch. "It looks like it's been dropped. The glass is cracked."

"Humph!" exploded Antonia crossly. "Why are people so lazy! It wouldn't have been difficult to take the torch ashore and put it in a bin."

"I know." Cai shoved the torch in the

pocket of his shorts. It was too big and the end stuck out, but at least it left his hands free to swim. "It's amazing down here. Shall we have a look round?"

Antonia and Cai spent a long while exploring the coral reef. It was fun watching tiny fish chasing each other in and out of the corals. Antonia liked the clownfish best, with their colourful orange and white scales. They saw a sea snake too. It slithered out from a crevice, swimming away from them, its black and silver striped body wiggling like a land snake.

"They're really poisonous," said Cai, shivering. "But luckily for us they're very shy and only bite if provoked."

All too soon it was time to leave. Reluctantly,

the Silver Dolphins followed Jet and Swirl to the surface. Diamond was waiting for them, but she wasn't cross that they'd been gone so long. Her liquid eyes sparkled and she opened her mouth in a wide smile.

"We've worked you hard, Silver Dolphins. Now it's time for some fun."

With a friendly nose rub Diamond said goodbye, then left the Silver Dolphins to play with her nephew and niece.

"Let's have a game of Sprat," said Jet. "I'll be it. It's a two-wave head start."

Determined not to get caught so easily this time, Antonia sped away. Swirl swam after her and giggling together they hid behind a cluster of rocks on the seabed. It was a fast game and everyone got caught at least twice.

Then Cai called a halt, begging Jet to teach him more dolphin tricks.

"How about this?" asked Jet, launching his body out of the water until he was standing on the surface on his tail. Faster than lightning he turned a full circle then splashed down into the sea, showering everyone with water.

"That's easy," clicked Antonia. She threw herself upwards and, copying Jet, turned a perfect twister of her own.

"Hooray!" cheered Cai. "My turn now." He practised the twister until he was turning full circles too. Then there was an enormous water fight with Antonia and Swirl taking on Cai and Jet. Soon the sea looked like a whirlpool; Antonia and Cai splashing with

their hands and the dolphins splashing with tails and fins.

"Truce!" panted Cai, stopping to shove the broken dive torch deeper in his pocket. "We should be getting home."

"We need to phone the North Coast Sea Life Rescue Charity to tell them about the turtles," Antonia remembered.

"Aw," sighed Jet. "Do you have to go right now?"

"The Silver Dolphins don't live here. Soon they'll go away for good," clicked Swirl sadly.

"But you'll come back, won't you?" asked Jet.

"Maybe," said Cai hopefully.

"I hope so," Antonia agreed. It would be great to come back and see the dolphins and the turtles too. But the holiday wasn't over yet. "Who's up for a last game of Sprat?" she asked.

"Me!" was the unanimous reply.

"I'll be it then. Ready or not... I'm coming!"

The sea was empty. Taking a deep breath Antonia dived down to find her friends.

by Summer Waters

*Buy more great Silver Dolphins books from HarperCollins
at 10% off recommended retail price. FREE postage and
packing in the UK.*

Out Now: